jE COX Robert
The platypus who couldn't
swi
Co
D1108418

OCT 1 7 2022

Robert Cox & Jim Robins

THE PLATYPUS who couldn't SWIM

REDBACK publishing

First Published 2021 by
Redback Publishing
PO Box 357 Frenchs Forest
NSW 2086
Australia

www.redbackpublishing.com

email: orders@redbackpublishing.com

© Redback Publishing 2021

ISBN: 978-1-922322-55-5

Author: Robert Cox
Illustrator: James Robins

Text copyright © Robert Cox 2021

Illustrations copyright © James Robins 2021

All rights reserved. No part of this publication may be reproduced, stored in a retrieval system or transmitted in any form or by any means, electronic, mechanical, photocopying, recording or otherwise, without the prior written permission of the publisher. All enquiries should be made to the publisher.

Printed and bound in China.

NATIONAL LIBRARY OF AUSTRALIA

A catalogue record for this book is available from the National Library of Australia

Dedicated to:
Mum, Dad & brother Alan. R.C
Ben, Tom & Nell. J.R

Beside a cool clear river
on the east coast of Australia,
a group of young platypuses
splashed happily in the water.

All except one.

They were singing a song that some of them found hilarious.
And some didn't.

"Poor Penny Platypus
Cannot swim a stroke
Scaredy Penny Platypus
What a silly joke!"

Penny watched them sadly,
wishing she wasn't frightened of the water.
Wishing she was brave and could join in.
Wishing she was like them.

But even worse than being **terrified** of the water, was being **terrified** of not knowing **WHY** she was **terrified**.

All she knew in her muddled head was that from the first time she slid off the bank and water covered her bill, she began sinking – and thought she would drown.

She'd **panicked** – and never tried again.

"Why can't I swim like them?" she would think over and over.

She would even dream about swimming and joining in the games. Dream about hunting her own food in the river instead of having it brought to her.

Fortunately, she had a best friend.
Percy.

"Don't worry," Percy would say cheerfully,
"one day it'll just happen. You'll see!"

But she also had a worst enemy.
Lucretia.

Lucretia had the loudest voice and had
made up the horrible song.

"Poor little Penny," she would whisper in Penny's ear
whenever she saw her, *"cannot swim a stroke."*

All the other platypuses were as frightened of Lucretia
as Penny was of the water, so they felt they had to laugh along
when they didn't want to.

Percy was **different**.

He wasn't frightened of **anyone**.

The months went by and the young platypuses were growing up quickly.

Percy brought Penny's food, as he did every day, and smiled at her.

"What about ...?" he said,

"... we go for a walk along the riverbank."

"Why?" asked Penny.

"Because," said Percy, "there's a little beach where you can sit safely in the shallow water. If you get used to that – with your feet and tummy on the ground but your bill, head and tail in the air – you might one day feel confident enough to swim."

Penny thought for a while, then said excitedly, **"Lets go!"**

She wanted to learn so much, and trusted
Percy completely.

Soon she was **shaking** with fear,
with water half-way up her body.

But Percy had put himself on the river side
of where she lay, so she couldn't slide in.

Suddenly he **frowned**
at her front claws in the water.

"Penny," he said, "**unfold your webs**."

"They are unfolded," replied Penny, shyly.

"No, they're not," said Percy, lifting one of his from the water. **"Look. That's unfolded!"**

And sure enough, the web between his claws meant he could spread them for swimming. But Penny didn't have a web, **just claws**.

"That's why you can't swim!" he cried, gently holding her claw and looking underneath. "You **HAVE** got webs. They just need to unfold, that's all. Go on, try."

Penny tried, and tried, and tried – but her webs just wouldn't unfold. **She started to cry.**

"That means," she said, "that I'll **never** be able to swim.

Never!

And Lucretia will sing that horrible song for ever more!"

"Oh no she won't," said Percy fiercely.
"Don't you worry. We'll sort it out."

He didn't know how
– but he didn't tell Penny he didn't know how.
He was just sure that one day they'd find a solution.

That was Percy – always looking on the bright side.

One week later was the
Platypus Annual Olympics.

Events included crawl, backstroke, butterfly (not easy for a platypus), the Egg-on-Bill race, and fetching a rock off the bottom of the river using the amazing radar system in their bills.

Platypuses have poor eyesight, but a highly sensitive bill which is very important for finding food and avoiding danger.

Penny dreaded it. But she was there to cheer on Percy who was in every event.

Lucretia swam up to the bank where Penny hid, peeping from behind a bush.

Lucretia was practising her backstroke, at which she was a champion, and singing her favourite song in her sarcastic voice.

"Poor Penny Platypus
Cannot swim a stroke
Scaredy Penny Platypus
What a silly joke!"

The day was full of fun and laughter, until the final event
– fetching a rock from the bottom of the river.
Whoever was fastest was the winner.

Percy was in the lead, with only Lucretia
left to dive. She lay on the riverbank,
waving to the crowd.

But then
something unexpected
happened.

Lucretia was so busy showing off, that she **slipped**.
Down, down she fell into the water,
close to where Penny was hiding behind a bush.

Nobody took any notice, thinking it was just
Lucretia being Lucretia, doing a fancy dive as usual.
But after a minute she hadn't appeared.

Penny crept out and peered cautiously
from the bank into the water. She could see Lucretia
tangled in weeds, **gasping** for air, her eyes **bulging**.

"**QUICK!**" she cried out,
"**Lucretia's drowning!**"

But, as she cried out, she lost her balance and fell in.

Down,
down,
down,

she fell, to where Lucretia's eyes and mouth were opening and closing, opening and closing.

When suddenly, in her panic – a miracle!
Penny's webs unfolded!

She **flapped**
and **flapped**
and **flapped** until,
wonder of wonders ...
she was
swimming!

Desperately, without thinking, she clawed at the weeds knotted around Lucretia, and soon had her free.

Then, with a stupendous effort, she pushed her upwards

- once,
twice,
three times

- until they both **burst** from the water!

Suddenly, Percy
was in the water
beside her.

"I've got her, Penny! Save yourself!" he shouted,
"Save yourself!"
Penny let go of Lucretia and swam to the bank.

And as she sat there
gasping, she looked
down at her claws
and spread
them **apart**.

She had
WEBS!

They were there all the time! Just stuck since she was born!

Then she heard cheering, **louder and louder!**
Lucretia had her arms around her, thanking her
and begging for forgiveness.

Penny looked at Lucretia calmly,
lifted her claws and showed her wide-open webs.

"No, thank **you** Lucretia! Now I can swim!
**It's the happiest day
of my life!**"

That evening, there were great celebrations.

Penny's life had changed forever.

The next day she and Percy went back to
the little beach further down the riverbank.

Percy was exhausted after the previous
day's exercise, and soon dozed off.

Penny watched as he slowly started sliding
into the water – and moved in front of him.

Percy felt her touch and woke up, surprised to see they had moved. But Penny just smiled and whispered ...

"It's okay Percy.
Go back to sleep.

I was just making sure
you don't fall in."